Jiu-Jitsu Jim

Story and Pictures
by
Daniel Thomas

https://amazon.com/author/dtpoet

https://twitter.com/DThomas_author

For my boys

Daddy loves you so much

Jim loves going to school. He loves reading new books and playing with his friends. He really enjoys learning lots of new things about the world.

Jim especially loves going home and telling his mom, dad and brother about his day. After dinner most nights Jim and his dad wrestle and play. His dad shows him and his brother lots of cool stuff.

Jim's favorite thing to do with his dad is learn Jiu-Jitsu. Jiu-Jitsu is really fun. Jim learns how to tackle his dad to the ground!

He learns how to hold on for dear life to his dad's back without falling off. This is his favorite Jiu-Jitsu move! What a ride!

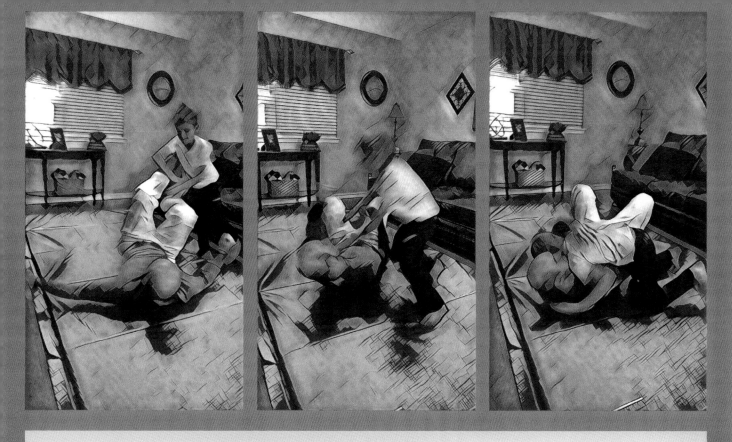

He also learns how to slip past his dad's wild legs and hold him from the side. Don't let go, Jiu-Jitsu Jim!

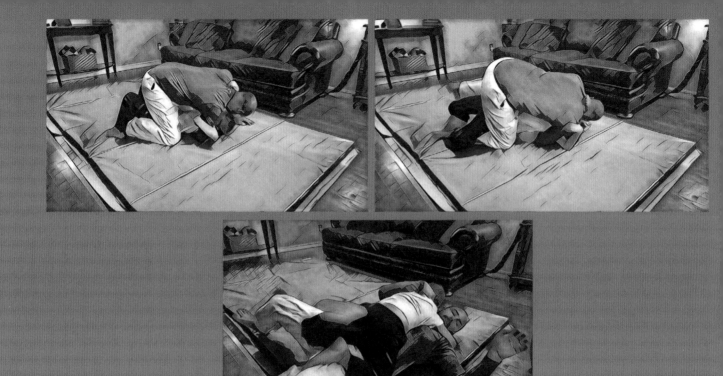

Then he learns that someone putting him in a headlock can work against them. Look at him flip his dad over! He really loves laughing and playing with his dad!

Jim's dad teaches him that Jiu-Jitsu is really fun, but also important. Jim is learning Jiu-Jitsu to protect himself and not to hurt other people. He must have the courage and discipline to use these skills wisely and for good.

Jim promises he will only use Jiu-Jitsu to protect himself. His dad tells him it is best that he never really need to use Jiu-Jitsu. Avoiding confrontation is the ultimate goal. The world is a much better place when people respect and care for their neighbor.

Jim jumps in the air and gives his dad a big bear hug. One of his favorite non-Jiu-Jitsu moves! (Though you could probably turn it into one.)

Now it's time to practice with brother. Roll on, Jiu-Jitsu Jim!

The End

About the Author

Daniel Thomas has written poetry since his youth and enjoys reading, sports, spending time with his family and perusing used book stores. He loves the writings of C. S. Lewis and Old Poets along with black and white films. Find more of his books on his Amazon author page. https://amazon.com/author/dtpoet

Printed in Great Britain
by Amazon